Alison McGhee

Illustrated by Sean Qualls

A CAITLYN DLOUHY BOOK
ATHENEUM BOOKS FOR YOUNG READERS
NEW YORK LONDON TORONTO SYDNEY NEW DELHI

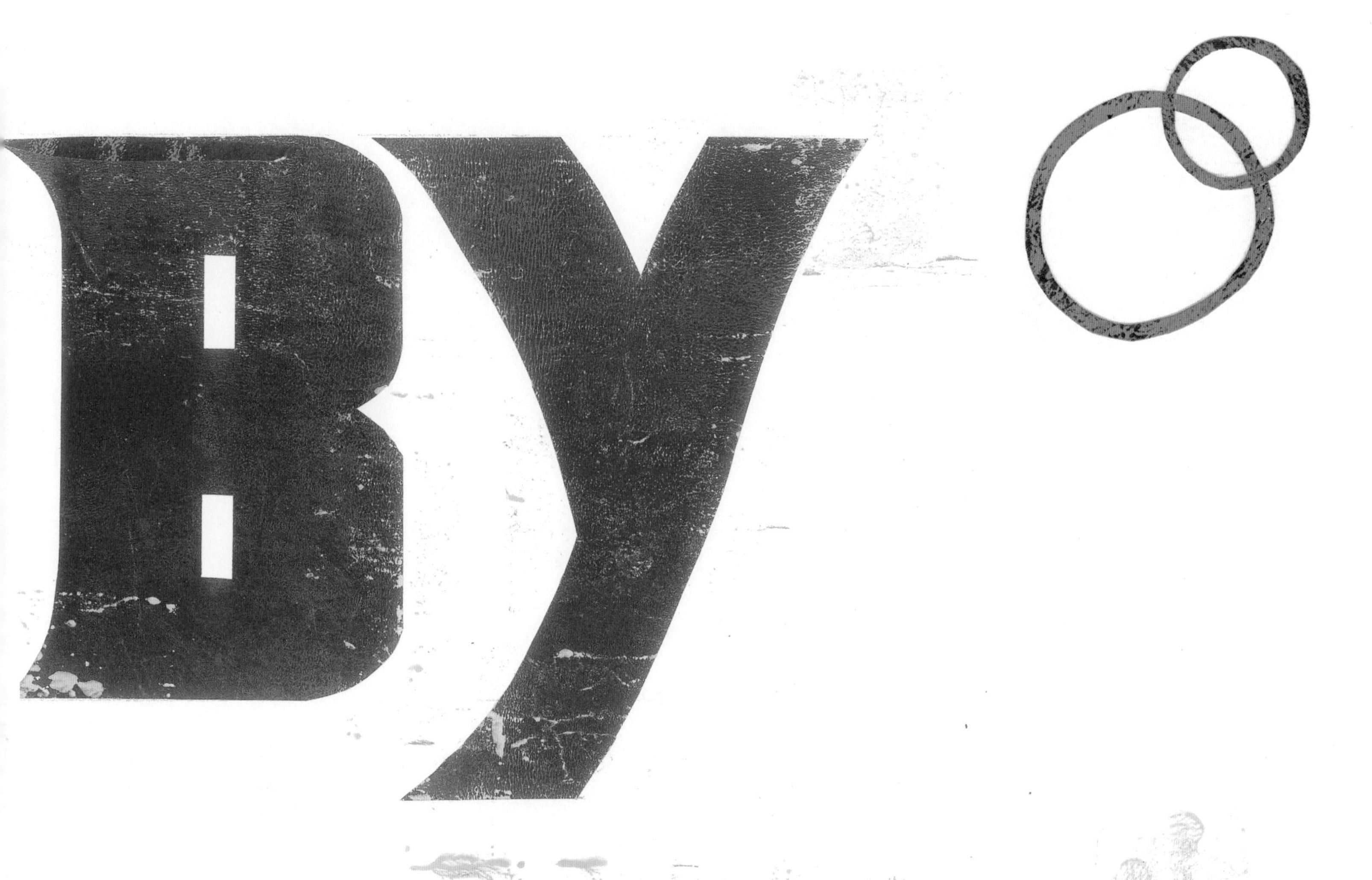
BY

BE

BABY!

High
five!

Down
low!

You ready?
Let's go!

Give me that tie

and I'll tie you
a bow,

give me your foot

and I'll
give you
my toe.

Your
drumming,

my strumming.

Your
beats.

My treats.

BABY!
You show me your
drop;

I'll show you my . . . flop.

Your grand plié,
my petit jeté.

Your sand and shovel,

my pop and scuffle.

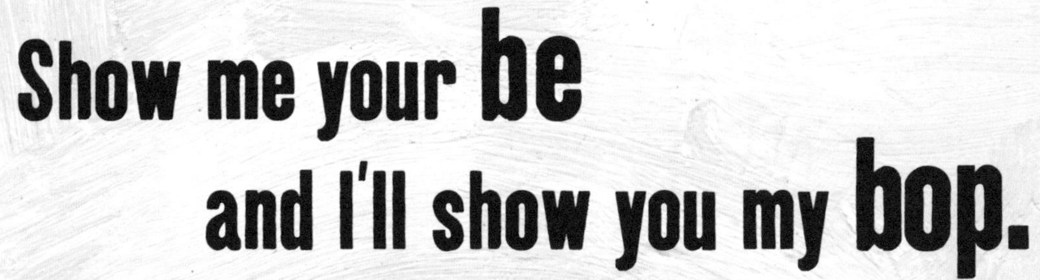
Show me your be
and I'll show you my bop.

BABY!
Give me
your hand
and we'll strike up the band.

We'll have us
a ball

and
I'll give you
my all.

My wiggle,
your woggle.

My swing
and your zing.

My boogie,
your woogie,
SUPER
DAD

my heart
and
its beat.

And all of my
days
and all of my
nights,

for the rest
of my life.

Wherever you are
and
whoever you'll be,

just know
that you're
already

perfect to me.

My baby,
oh baby,
oh baby,
just . . .
BE.

To Brandon Reader
and all the other
joyous dads out
there—A. M.

For the one and only
Isaiah Qualls,
with love—S. Q.

atheneum

ATHENEUM BOOKS FOR YOUNG READERS
An imprint of Simon & Schuster Children's Publishing Division
1230 Avenue of the Americas, New York, New York 10020 | | For information about special discounts for bulk
purchases, please contact Simon & Schuster Special Sales at 1-866-506-1949 or business@
simonandschuster.com. | The Simon & Schuster Speakers Bureau can bring authors to your live event.
For more information or to book an event, contact the Simon & Schuster Speakers Bureau at
1-866-248-3049 or visit our website at www.simonspeakers.com. | The text for this book was set in Kipp
Offc and Cachet Pro. | The illustrations for this book were rendered in acrylic paint, colored pencil, and
collage. | Manufactured in China | 0623 SCP First Edition | 10 9 8 7 6 5 4 3 2 1 | Library of Congress
Cataloging-in-Publication Data | Names: McGhee, Alison, 1960- author. Qualls, Sean, illustrator. Title: Baby be
/ Alison McGhee ; illustrated by Sean Qualls. Description: First edition. | New York : Atheneum Books for Young
Readers, 2023. | "A Caitlyn Dlouhy Book." | Audience: Ages 4-8. | Audience: Grades K-1. | Summary: As they
dance, wiggle, and boogie together, fathers assure their sons that they can become anything they want and
that they will always have their fathers' support | Identifiers: LCCN 2020047748 | ISBN 9781534405394
(hardcover) | ISBN 9781534405400 (ebook) | Subjects: CYAC: Stores in rhyme. Fathers and sons—
Fiction. | Love—Fiction. Dance—Fiction. Classification: LCC PZ8.3.M45956 Bab 2023 |
DDC [E]—dc23 | LC record available at https://lccn.loc.gov/2020047748